THE TALE OF
PETER RABBIT

BY BEATRIX POTTER

FREDERICK WARNE

ONCE upon a time there were four little Rabbits, and their names were—Flopsy, Mopsy, Cotton-tail, and Peter.

They lived with their Mother in a sand-bank, underneath the root of a very big fir-tree.

"NOW, my dears," said old Mrs. Rabbit one morning, "you may go into the fields or down the lane, but don't go into Mr. McGregor's garden. Your Father had an accident there; he was put in a pie by Mrs. McGregor."

"NOW run along, and don't get
into mischief. I am going out."
  Then old Mrs. Rabbit took a
basket and her umbrella, and
went through the wood to the
baker's. She bought a loaf of
brown bread and five
currant buns.

8

FLOPSY, Mopsy, and Cotton-tail, who were good little bunnies, went down the lane to gather blackberries;

BUT Peter, who was very naughty, ran straight away to Mr. McGregor's garden, and squeezed under the gate!

FIRST he ate some lettuces and some French beans; and then he ate some radishes;

AND then, feeling rather sick, he went to look for some parsley.

BUT round the end of a cucumber frame, whom should he meet but Mr. McGregor!

Mr. McGregor was on his hands and knees planting out young cabbages, but he jumped up and ran after Peter, waving a rake and calling out, "Stop thief!"

PETER was most dreadfully frightened; he rushed all over the garden, for he had forgotten the way back to the gate.

He lost one of his shoes among the cabbages, and the other shoe amongst the potatoes.

AFTER losing them, he ran on four legs and went faster, so that I think he might have got away altogether if he had not unfortunately run into a gooseberry net, and got caught by the large buttons on his jacket. It was a blue jacket with brass buttons, quite new.

PETER gave himself up for lost, and shed big
tears; but his sobs were overheard by some friendly
sparrows, who flew to him in great excitement, and
implored him to exert himself.

MR. McGREGOR came up with a sieve, which he intended to pop upon the top of Peter; but Peter wriggled out just in time, leaving his jacket behind him.

AND rushed into the tool-shed, and jumped into a can. It would have been a beautiful thing to hide in, if it had not had so much water in it.

Mr. McGregor was quite sure that Peter was somewhere in the tool-shed, perhaps hidden underneath a flower-pot. He began to turn them over carefully, looking under each.

Presently Peter sneezed—"Kertyschoo!" Mr. McGregor was after him in no time,

AND tried to put his foot upon Peter, who jumped out of a window, upsetting three plants. The window was too small for Mr. McGregor, and he was tired of running after Peter. He went back to his work.

PETER sat down to rest; he was out of breath and trembling with fright, and he had not the least idea which way to go. Also he was very damp with sitting in that can.

After a time
he began to
wander about,
going lippity—
lippity—not
very fast, and
looking all
round.

HE found a door in a wall; but it was locked, and there was no room for a fat little rabbit to squeeze underneath.

An old mouse was running in and out over the stone door-step, carrying peas and beans to her family in the wood. Peter asked her the way to the gate, but she had such a large pea in her mouth that she could not answer. She only shook her head at him. Peter began to cry.

THEN he tried
to find his way
straight across
the garden, but
he became more
and more puzzled.
Presently, he came
to a pond where
Mr. McGregor
filled his water-
cans. A white cat
was staring at some

gold-fish; she sat very, very still, but now and then
the tip of her tail twitched as if it were alive. Peter
thought it best to go away without speaking to
her; he had heard about cats from his cousin, little
Benjamin Bunny.

HE went back towards the tool-shed, but suddenly, quite close to him, he heard the noise of a hoe—scr-r-ritch, scratch, scratch, scritch. Peter scuttered underneath the bushes. But presently, as nothing happened, he came out, and climbed upon a wheelbarrow and peeped over. The first thing he saw was Mr. McGregor hoeing onions. His back was turned towards Peter, and beyond him was

the gate!

Peter got down very quietly off the wheelbarrow, and started running as fast as he could go, along a straight walk behind some black-currant bushes.

MR. McGREGOR caught sight of him at the corner, but Peter did not care. He slipped underneath the gate, and was safe at last in the wood outside the garden.

MR. McGREGOR hung up the little jacket
and the shoes for a scarecrow to frighten the
blackbirds.

PETER never stopped running or looked behind
him till he got home to the big fir-tree.

He was so tired that he flopped down upon
the nice soft sand on the floor of the rabbit-hole
and shut his eyes. His mother was busy cooking;
she wondered what
he had done with
his clothes. It
was the second
little jacket
and pair of
shoes that
Peter had
lost in a
fortnight!

I AM sorry to say that Peter was not very well during the evening.

His mother put him to bed, and made some camomile tea; and she gave a dose of it to Peter!

"One table-spoonful to be taken at bed-time."

BUT Flopsy, Mopsy, and Cotton-tail had bread and milk and blackberries for supper.

FREDERICK WARNE

Published by the Penguin Group
Registered office: 80 Strand, London, WC2R 0RL
Penguin Young Readers Group, 345 Hudson Street, New York, N.Y. 10014, USA

First published 1902 by Frederick Warne
This edition with new reproductions of Beatrix Potter's book illustrations first published 2006
This edition copyright © Frederick Warne & Co. 2006
Reissued 2016
New reproductions of Beatrix Potter's book illustrations copyright © Frederick Warne & Co. 2002
Original copyright in text and illustrations © Frederick Warne & Co., 1902

Frederick Warne & Co. is the owner of all rights, copyrights and trademarks in the
Beatrix Potter character names and illustrations.

Manufactured in China

Special Markets ISBN 978-0-241-29829-9